Growing up, Nicola Franklin had dreams of becoming a cartoonist. She could spend hours with a pencil in hand scribbling away instead of doing her homework. Another of her favourite hobbies was (and still is) reading poetry, although she'd never made any attempt to write it. Then one day, she grabbed a pad and pen and decided to bring some of her quirky, animated comic characters into the world of rhyme.

Nicola Franklin

Funny Little Rhymes for Funny Little Kids

Austin Macauley Publishers
LONDON • CAMBRIDGE • NEW YORK • SHARJAH

Copyright © Nicola Franklin (2020)

The right of **Nicola Franklin** to be identified as author of this work has been asserted by her in accordance with section 77 and 78 of the Copyright, Designs and Patents Act 1988.

All rights reserved. No part of this publication may be reproduced, stored in a retrieval system, or transmitted in any form or by any means, electronic, mechanical, photocopying, recording, or otherwise, without the prior permission of the publishers.

Any person who commits any unauthorised act in relation to this publication may be liable to criminal prosecution and civil claims for damages.

A CIP catalogue record for this title is available from the British Library.

ISBN 9781528909952 (Paperback)
ISBN 9781528909969 (Hardback)
ISBN 9781528959445 (ePub e-book)
www.austinmacauley.com

First Published (2020)
Austin Macauley Publishers Ltd
25 Canada Square
Canary Wharf
London
E14 5LQ

DANNY THE SNAIL

Under a hedge in someone's back garden
sits a funny brown rock
with a tail, but it's really a shell,
a tiny round house and inside it
lives Danny the snail.

Since the day he was born,
he has stayed in the warm,
never venturing outside his home.
But Danny feels bored,
'cos there's no one to play with,
he's grown tired of being alone.

So suddenly brave, he plucks up the courage
to poke his slimy round-head out the door.
Feeling triumphant, like a beast in the wild,
he lets out a lion like roar.

His adventure begins and it starts with a biscuit
left shimmering out in the sun.
This sugary treat, that's crunchy to eat,
gives Danny his first taste of fun.
But uh-oh, a dog starts chasing poor Danny
and is trying to gobble him up,
But one lick with his tongue,
the hound turns tail to run
because snails taste slimy and

YUK!!!

Danny comes to a slide and squeaks up the side,
wondering what there is up there to see.
When he gets to the top, he loses his balance
and slides all the way down shouting,

"WEEEEEEE!!!"

"Hello, what's your name?
I'm Cecil the worm,"
comes a small friendly voice from the grass.
"I'm Danny the snail, from under the hedge,
you might see me sometimes as you pass."

"I'm sure I have," smiles Cecil, now thinking,
"you're the funny brown rock with a tail,
I'd never have guessed it, I'd never have known,
that it turns out you're really a snail."

"I've come out to play, it's my very first day,
and I'm happy to find some new mates."
As Danny explains, Cecil's buddies creep over,
with two rather curious snakes.

There's a ladybird, Lily, a spider called Frank
and a centipede named Mr Plum,
"But avoid Wayne the wasp," Cecil warns Danny,
"if you don't, you'll be horribly stung."

But Wayne spots Danny and is tearing towards him,
his sting is as sharp as a spike.
So Danny retreats and hides in his shell,
and poor Wayne is knocked out like a light.

The wasp has been beaten and bumped on the head,
the creatures all shout out and cheer,
"Danny, you did it, come out of your shell,
there's no need to hide out in fear."
So Danny pops out, and they all walk about,
until they find somewhere
shaded to settle.
There by a tree sits a little red mushroom
shrouded by two giant nettles.

"We'll be safe under here," says Frank,
bounding up and perching himself on the top.
He starts weaving a web
above everyone's heads
and ties himself up in a knot.

Mr Plum sits beside and lets out a sigh,
quite grateful the sun is so hot.
"I don't like the cold," he says, shaking his
legs, "because I have to wear hundreds of socks."

Then Lilly flies up as red as the roses,
but wishes sometimes she was green.
"Children with jars come searching the grass,
so at least then I wouldn't be seen."

They spot a balloon on the tree branch above,
just tied up and left there to hang.
They give it a clout and bat it about,
until it bursts with an ear-splitting bang.

Danny gets scared and wants to go home,
setting both of the snakes hissing.
"Danny, don't leave,"
laughs Cecil with Frank,
"just think of the things you'll be missing."

"The world is our oyster
and life's an adventure and it's not a big deal
that we're small.
Amid the big shoes, the mowers and trikes,
this garden's the kingdom we rule."

"There's candy to eat and creatures to meet
and shiny round marbles to roll.
The lawn is a treasure,
a world of its own
where little toy soldiers patrol."

So off Danny goes with his new set of friends,
and the ladybird gives him a kiss.
With the garden and more
for them all to explore,
it seems being a snail is bliss.

DOCTOR DOOM

Doctor Doom is our family doctor,
he's ninety-nine years old.
He's as wrinkled as a rotten prune
and his hands are icy cold.
He's six feet tall and his
nose is pointy, his body's as thin as a rake,
he's got glaring, staring bright green eyes
and a tongue just like a snake.
He wears a hat and long black coat
and shiny shoes that squeak.
He also wears some thick round glasses
perched upon his beak.
His skin's a faded shade of purple,
his hair is silver grey.
He smells of potent potions
and disinfectant spray.
He carries around a stethoscope
and a green prescription pad.
But the thing that really gives me chills
is that big black leather bag.
That dreaded bag that's filled with ointments,
medicines and pills, files and pencils,
sharp utensils and big electric drills.
You would think I'd hate the needles most
but the medicine's the worst.
It burns like poison going down,
'til my tonsils almost burst.
Doctor Doom is quite old fashioned,
he likes the old-school way, so I'm truly hoping
his thermometer's broken when he visits me today.

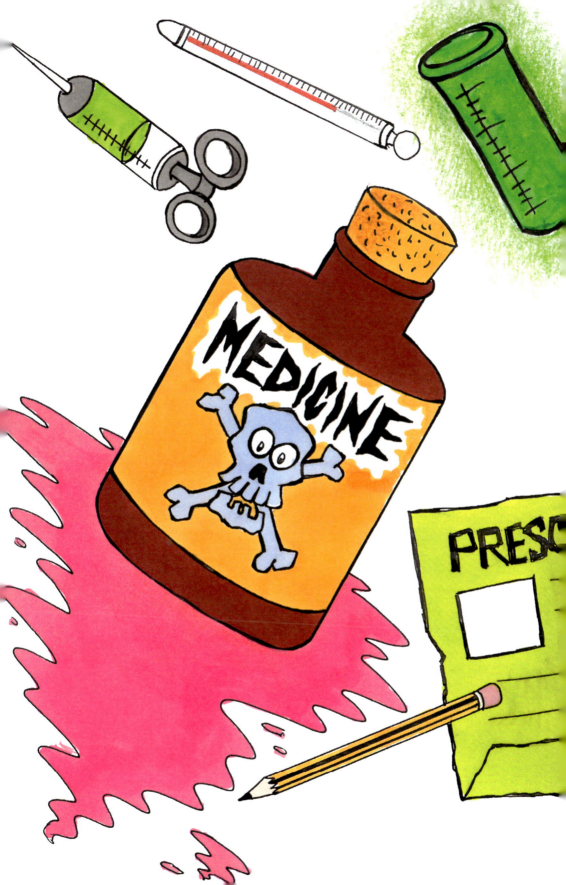

THE GHOST IN THE SHED

I think there's a ghost in the garden shed,
that big wooden hovel that fills me with dread.
It's a rotten, rickety, creepy old shack
that sits in the overgrown grass out the back.
Wrapped in the clutches of branches and strands,
like it's trapped in the clasp of skeletons hands.
It creaks and squeaks in the wind and rain,
like a howling werewolf screaming in pain.
Every night of the week I get rudely awoken
by the sound of the door as it creaks slowly open.
There's mysterious noises and loud heavy bumps,
repetitive knocking and unexplained thumps.
I wouldn't go into that shed
if you paid me
and I really don't care if
you think I'm a baby.
My mum thinks it's silly
and so does my dad.
I've tried to explain, but they both think I'm mad.
They say, "Why would a ghost
be haunting a shed,
when it could live in a house
and sleep warm in a bed."

But ghosts don't need houses
or warm comfy beds.
They like to haunt attics.
dark cellars and sheds,
and they don't need to sleep 'cos they're up half the night
scaring us all when we turn off the light.
Still, I don't think I need to worry about that
because our ghost is haunting
that spooky old shack.
It will stay in the shed
where it's dutifully bound
and haunt it for years until…
Wait, what's that sound?

CREEEEAAAAK!

Was that the shed door?
It sounds so much closer,
like it's under the floor.
But it couldn't be coming
from anywhere close.
What's that in the hall?

OH CRIPES, IT'S A GHOST!

NANA'S LOST HER KNICKERS

NANA'S LOST HER KNICKERS

Nana's lost her knickers and we don't know what to do,
they fell right down in the middle of town,
then up and away they flew.
The wind had sent them flying,
high up into space, they collided with an alien,
wrapping tightly round his face.
They came back down to Earth again
and drifted on the breeze,
but while they enjoyed their freedom,
Nan's butt began to freeze.

A tourist took a picture as they flew across Penzance.
Is it a bird?
Is it a plane?
No, it's a massive pair of pants.
They landed on a river then bubbled up and sank,
a passing fish was so disgusted, he threw them on the bank.
A bird swooped by and picked them up,
and flew them back to town.
He gave a tweet in a crowded street,
then slowly set them down.

They covered half the bus lane, and people stopped to stare,
then wild ferocious laughter loudly filled the air.
But at least Nan had her knickers back,
as we peeled them off the road,
even though she had to share them now
with an eel and several toads.

THERE'S A GOAT ON THE BOAT

Today, we went out boating,
sailing on the sea,
my mum and dad, my brother and
sister, my gran, the dog and me.
We thought we'd have a break
today, from working on the farm,
feeding the pigs, milking the cows
and cleaning out the barn.
So ready or not, we got on the yacht
and sped across the water.
The engine roaring, full steam ahead,
we raced a mile and a quarter.
We took along a picnic lunch,
packed up in a box, we also packed a towel each
and a nice clean pair of socks.
But when we stopped to have a bite,
we couldn't believe our eyes.
The box was ransacked, ripped to shreds,
like a bomb went off inside.
Barney took the blame at first,
we always blame the dog,
'cos he eats the post and digs the garden
and slurps water from the bog.
My gran was feeling seasick,
swaying on the boat,
so my sister opened the bathroom door
and stood there was our goat.
It had chocolate around its hairy chin
and was chewing on a sock.
My sister screamed, my brother laughed
and my mum passed out from shock.

It ran upstairs and my dad gave a chase
and trapped it on the deck,
then I raced up with Barney's lead
to tie around its neck.
It wriggled about and kicked its way free,
and butted my dad in the nose.
It chewed through his hair,
like a barber's razor,
and gobbled its way through his clothes.
Then Gran, still feeling seasick,
came outside for air.
She leaned across the safety rail
and the poor thing lost her hair.
Her wig fell in the water
and drifted out to sea,
but there was nothing I could do to help,
'cos the goat was chasing me.
Up and down and round and round,
then I found a place to hide.
So the goat ran back and charged at Gran
and knocked her off the side.
We hauled her in and pulled her up,
she was soaked from top to toe.
She threw a fish at my dad and screamed,

"THAT GOAT HAS GOT TO GO!"

But it already had, it was sailing away
on the back of a great white shark.
We chased it but the sun had set
and we lost it in the dark.
So that was the end of the goat
on the boat,
or at least that's what we thought,
'cos when we got home, a fisherman
knocked and showed us what he'd caught.
Our goat was rescued safe and sound,
though tangled in a net.
My gran was bald and angry still,
but at least she wasn't wet.

THE MAGIC OF NIGHT

We often miss the magic of night,
when we lay in bed with our eyes shut tight.
We miss the owls hooting gently in the trees,
we miss the moon shining brightly through the leaves.
We miss how it glows when the clouds waft past,
so never do we see the clever shadows it can cast.
We miss the little hedgehogs waddling around,
sniffing every pebble as they creep along the ground.
We even miss the bats in flight,
those creepy little monsters and keepers of the night.
We miss the distant howling dog and the eerie reflections of
thick swirling fog.
So when everything's quiet and everything's still,
have a quick peek over your window sill,
or you might just miss the magic of night,
if you lay in bed with your eyes shut tight.